HYACINTH

Published by Casuals Network Press
Naarm, Australia

ISBN 978-0-9942251-5-3

Text © Will Cox 2023

Print-on-demand edition

Typeset in Caslon Pro
Cover illustration: 'The Death of Hyacinth' by Alexander Kiselyov
Public domain image via Wikimedia Commons

Printed on recycled paper by Eureka Printing, Glen Waverley

This book was produced on the traditional lands of the Wurundjeri people of the Kulin nation. We pay our respects to their Elders, past and present. Sovereignty was never ceded.

HYACINTH

a story by

WILL COX

For Charlotte

The Honey

Elizabeth visits her neighbour Hyacinth for morning tea. Hyacinth serves her scones and jam and honey, and tea in a special plastic mug that Elizabeth can't break. The phone rings, and Hyacinth rushes out of the room to answer it. She calls out from the hallway—it's her son, Sheridan. Startled, Elizabeth accidentally knocks the jar of honey to the floor. It shatters. Hyacinth rushes back in, drops to her knees, and tries to mop it up with her hands. Elizabeth puts her hand on Hyacinth's shoulder and tells her to stop. Hyacinth slows, and begins to sob. She grips Elizabeth's hand, which becomes sticky with honey, and bloody from small shards of glass.

That night Hyacinth's sleep is interrupted by a buzzing sound in the bedroom. She tries to wake Richard but she can't move. Above her head floats a baby with the wings of a fly, dripping a viscous, sweet-smelling liquid.

In the morning, Hyacinth wakes to find the bedsheets are covered in honey.

Please Mind Your Head

Hyacinth and Richard have spent their savings on a property in the countryside. Hyacinth has been envisioning a rambling Georgian cottage, snaked tastefully with vines, with flowerbeds to tend and a formal sitting room in which to entertain. When they arrive, she's disappointed to find that it's small—far smaller than it seemed at the inspection—more like a large shed, with low ceilings and tiny doors. It seems to get smaller every time she looks around.

They wake in the night to find the walls pressing in on the bed, the timber frame groaning beneath them. They hear a snap, and they scramble out of bed as it buckles. Just in time, they manage to squeeze out the tiny front door. Hyacinth turns and watches as the cottage shrinks to the size of a doll's house. Eventually, it disappears entirely.

Left to wander through the dark and strange forest to find their car, Richard worries about the insurance on a disappearing house.

Singing For Emmet

ELIZABETH'S BROTHER, EMMET, IS HIDING. HOPING TO GET A ROLE in Emmet's new musical, Hyacinth has been watching the house and singing show tunes at him whenever he walks out the front door. Emmet hasn't left the house for a week.

Elizabeth encourages him to stand up to her and say he's already cast the show.

It's not that simple, says Emmet. We're trapped. And our lives are just a series of little embarrassments.

Elizabeth knows this. She has come to realise that everyone in their world—all over fifty, lonely, and terrified—is held firm by the sheer force of Hyacinth's will.

Hyacinth has a powerful core of anger, says Elizabeth. One with its own gravitational pull.

Recently divorced Emmet replies: Just being alive is to be caught in someone else's orbit. First my wife's. Now Hyacinth's. It's pointless to resist.

Emmet begins composing a new song. It's about a houseboat sailing through an ocean of flowers. He has no idea what to do with it.

Sea Fever

HYACINTH AND RICHARD TAKE A BOATING HOLIDAY ON A CANAL outside Bath. Hyacinth invites Elizabeth and Emmet to come, but they cancel at the last minute, leaving Hyacinth to wonder just what it is about her that makes people feel the need to avoid her.

They hire a canal barge. On the water, Hyacinth reminisces about her childhood on a ramshackle houseboat with her Daddy and sisters, Violet, Daisy, and Rose. It was an idyllic youth, she says. That night, as the water lulls around her, she dreams of steering the ship towards land, breaking apart the banks, and sailing through cracked earth out onto a sea of Champagne. Sunset hits, and the tide swells. On the horizon, she sees Sheridan's face. It's just as she remembers it. But just as she calls out his name, his features dissolve into the honey sunset.

Senior Citizens' Outing

Hyacinth asks Richard about the people in the house. Has he seen them too?

When she, Richard, and Sheridan first moved into this house, decades ago, Hyacinth had the notion that there was an old couple still living there. She never saw them, but she felt them, in the air, behind her, around corners. There was never a feeling of solitude. There was always somebody else there. Eventually, the old people left. Or perhaps Hyacinth just became accustomed to filtering them out, like the low hiss of a detuned radio.

Now, she is worried they've returned. She feels echoes around her, feels breath. Feels the somethingness of a presence in the room.

It's an old building, Richard says. These things happen.

It's not that old, says Hyacinth.

That night while brushing her teeth, Hyacinth sees a shadow moving outside the bathroom window. She freezes. It's just her reflection. But there, out of the corner of her eye again, a flicker of movement at the bathroom window. It's past ten, but it seems to be light outside. Hyacinth opens the window and peers through.

Behind the frosted glass is another room, similar to her own bathroom. The wallpaper, the decor, the layout, are all the same, but mirrored, dimly lit. Standing at the vanity unit, a young woman stares back at her, toothpaste dripping from her open mouth. The young woman is Hyacinth herself, thirty years younger. Young Hyacinth screams, drops her toothbrush, and runs from the room.

Old Hyacinth slams the window shut and locks it.

Neither Hyacinth tells Richard.

Angel Gabriel Blue

In town, Hyacinth picks out new fittings and bench tops for her dream kitchen. Sheridan's cot was blue, she remembers. Angel Gabriel Blue. That was the colour of the cot shown in the brochure, and that was the colour she chose. She will choose it again.

Hyacinth invites Elizabeth over for morning tea. On the kitchen table, she has laid out her kitchen plans. Elizabeth excuses herself and, on her way to the bathroom, finds a doorway she's never seen before. Through it, there is a long corridor. The walls of the corridor are lined with the same striped beige wallpaper as the rest of Hyacinth's house. She follows the winding hallway to its end. There's another door, ajar. Through the gap, Elizabeth sees blazing sunlight, and hears a baby crying. She doesn't enter.

When she finds her way back to the kitchen, it's dark outside and the house is still. Hyacinth's snores echo through the house.

Hyacinth dreams of the Archangel Gabriel—tall, broad-shouldered, his gown a perfect shade of blue. He's cradling her baby. His oversized wings scrape her hallway walls, leaving behind smears of honey.

Ring Road

AFTER CHURCH ON SUNDAY, HYACINTH INSISTS RICHARD DRIVE around the block again so that Mrs Councillor Nugent can see her hat. Lost in a tangle of one-way streets, they take an exit onto a highway and find themselves several lanes deep on a ring road. Hyacinth consults a map, but she can't seem to place them. They drive for hours, unable to find an exit.

Long into the night they are still driving, the silver moon hanging bright overhead. Richard worries about running out of petrol. Hyacinth realises that under the moonlight it appears that none of the other cars have drivers, just empty seats. It's morning before the drivers reappear in their vehicles, and a woman in a white Mini Metro slows to allow them to merge and take the last exit back to suburbia.

Rose meets a new gentleman friend, Mr White, who lives in a bedsit above the tea shop and has a voice like the soft ring of a prayer bell. She falls deeply in love.

Skis

Hyacinth has bought Richard skis for his birthday because they 'will look good on the car'. As they drive to her sister Violet's to borrow a roof rack, Hyacinth spies Elizabeth coming out of Waitrose with two overfull plastic shopping bags. She insists that Richard stop and pick her up. In the car, it becomes clear to Elizabeth that she is not being offered a lift home.

Violet has a charming estate, says Hyacinth. I'm sure they'll invite us to stay for high tea.

Violet's house is a mansion surrounded by gardens, hidden behind wrought-iron gates. The sign says *The Paddocks*. There's no one in, but the doors are unlocked. While Richard and Hyacinth struggle with the roof rack, Elizabeth goes into the house to see if she can put her shopping in the fridge. The house is vast and dark, and the grand rooms are dominated by huge paintings of horses.

Footsteps startle Elizabeth. Bruce, Violet's husband, walks into the kitchen. But he's calm, kind, and puts her immediately at ease.

Over tea—of which she doesn't spill a drop—Elizabeth asks him about the horse decor. Bruce tells her that when he was a boy, he was charged and trampled by a horse. He would summer at his father's stables, the only time they spent together. One afternoon, Bruce saw his father repeatedly kicking an injured thoroughbred.

Bruce describes his father's boot going in again and again, until he turned and saw him. He had pure rage in his eyes, says Bruce. I just ran.

He climbed through a fence and into a paddock. Turning to see his father running towards him, Bruce collided with the back of a huge white stallion. The creature kicked, throwing him against the wooden fence. When Bruce got up to run away the stallion turned and charged, head down, front teeth bared. His feet wouldn't move. They were fixed to the ground as he felt the power of the animal coming towards him. The last thing Bruce remembers is his own reflection in the creature's glassy eyes.

He spent six months bedridden, and it was six months more before he could walk unaided.

As she sets down her teacup in the sink, Elizabeth asks why all the glassware in the cabinets is engraved with the names of jockeys.

Dead jockeys, says Bruce.

On her way out, Elizabeth steals a small porcelain bust of a horse.

The Sparrow Call

HYACINTH THINKS SHE HEARS THE POSTMAN, BUT WHEN SHE GOES outside to ask him how many envelopes he has for the neighbours across the road, there's no one there. There's only a tiny grey sparrow, dead on her welcome mat.

Overcome with tenderness, she brings the corpse inside, places it in an old biscuit tin lined with shredded paper, and prays in silence. Then she leaves the open tin on the bench, planning to bury it the following day.

In the morning, she comes into the kitchen to find the tin is empty. Just then, Hyacinth hears a rustling sound overhead. She looks around the room, but sees nothing. There's the noise again, by the door. She follows the sound around the house, and it becomes deafeningly loud: the sound of wings, and the call of a sparrow, close, all around her. But she never finds the bird.

So she tries to ignore it.

The Boy Friend

ROSE HAS TAKEN UP WITH MR WHITE, A BUSINESSMAN FROM OUT of town with a voice like a prayer bell. They spend all their free time together in his apartment, making love, drinking white wine, and laughing into the night. Daisy tries to talk her sister out of her new affair, but Rose is defiantly happy with her newfound sense of commitment.

I'm in love, cries Rose. I'm in deep. I can't escape it. I'm happier than I've ever been.

Love is something, says Daisy. Love is a nice story, but these stories are never good enough.

Onslow is woken in the night by Rose hauling a suitcase down the stairs. She tells him she's moving in with her Mr White.

Mr White is standing at the foot of the stairs, tall and thin, in a dark suit and a bowler hat. He has talc-white skin and dark eyes. He smiles broadly at Onslow, exposing yellow teeth. Onslow sees a bee crawl out of the corner of his mouth.

A Strange Man

DAISY TELLS HYACINTH SHE IS WORRIED ABOUT ROSE MOVING IN with her lover, Mr White.

No one around here knows him, she says, as Hyacinth perches on the edge of the dirty couch. He just turns up and takes our Rose away from us. It's not right.

Hyacinth suggests sending Richard to spy on him. Long ago, she explains, Richard was a spy for Her Majesty's Government. He often spent lengthy stints abroad, at all the best hotels, says Hyacinth, picking a tuft of dog hair from the couch arm.

When Hyacinth leaves the room, Richard clarifies that he wasn't actually staying in the hotels, but staking them out from the outside, in surveillance vans, gathering intel on the unsavoury sexual habits of wealthy businessmen and Soviet Bloc politicians.

In her new, empty apartment she shares with Mr White, Rose sleeps a deep, dreamless sleep.

Daddy dreams of an endless river, snaking through yellow sands.

Horse England

Bruce has a horse costume that he wears alone at night. He's trying to understand the beast's power. It's composed of a long, brown horse-hair cloak and a horse skull.

When Violet goes to sleep, Bruce dons the cloak and skull and trots around the wide, empty halls of his house, snuffling at the memories the house holds, all wet with Emotion. In the kitchen, Guilt. In the laundry, Desire. To wear the horse is to travel to a past—warm, dank, ever-living. In the skull he can hold a moment, study its energy. The horse lives in Past, in Feeling. It knows the roads and hills and canals there. Feeling is its England.

Bruce-as-horse rears up to a bouquet of fresh-cut flowers and inhales their green. A single stem can be a whole garden, foul with life. In a fit of Passion, Bruce-as-horse knocks the vase from its place on the sideboard, sending glass, water and flowers skimming across the floorboards.

Violet comes downstairs and asks Bruce to be a little quieter.

A Job for Richard

RICHARD BEGINS HIS STAKE-OUT OF MR WHITE'S APARTMENT. Mr White lives on the main street, over a tea shop. From behind the steering wheel, Richard finds the right room: a naked bulb illuminates the silhouette of a man, standing by the window, looking out. Is it Mr White? Is he looking directly at Richard? Is it a person at all? It's too hard to tell in this light.

After several hours of inaction Richard falls asleep. He dreams of a shore somewhere, gently glittering under the sun.

He hears laughter.

He picks up a shell.

He's woken by a sharp tap on the window. His eyes adjust to the figure leaning over him. It's Rose, wearing a dressing gown, cigarette between her fingers. He winds the window down.

Did our Hyacinth put you up to this? Rose asks.

Richard nods.

Well, you can sod off and tell her it's none of her business, she says.

Richard reaches for words but finds none. Rose stubs out her cigarette under her heel, and walks around the car to sit in the passenger seat.

She means well, Rose, says Richard.

Rose closes her eyes. The two sit in silence for some minutes, and then Rose tells Richard that when they were girls, all four of them shared a room in the houseboat. Richard says he knows that. But Rose says that Daddy would come home drunk and would often bring company.

He's always had an eye for the girls, has Daddy, she says.

On those nights, as the boat pitched and yawed, the four girls, the Walton girls, would lie awake in the dark, listening to the creaking of wood and the crescendo of voices through the thin wall.

We all took something different away from those nights, says Rose.

Young Hyacinth

Richard and Hyacinth have had sex precisely twice.

On their fourth date, Richard arrived at Hyacinth's apartment early, stood around the corner for fifteen minutes smoking nervously, and then stood at her door for another five minutes before he worked up the courage to knock. The apartment smelt of Dettol and flowers. Hyacinth served him roast beef and potatoes, red wine, and a chocolate pudding afterwards. She drank twice as fast as Richard, making nervous conversation about the royal family. Richard noticed several framed portraits of Queen Elizabeth around the room. When they finished eating, Hyacinth pushed the table against the wall and put on a Mantovani record. Richard and Hyacinth danced close and awkward, the swelling strings and her warm breath like syrup in his ears.

In the bedroom, Richard—young, quiet, not quite a virgin but not far off—held her in the dark, touched her through her nightgown, fumbled through motions that lasted only seconds. Immediately afterwards, Hyacinth ran to the bathroom and stayed there. Richard heard the door lock behind her. He lay there on her single bed, sweaty, ashamed, staring at the light under the bathroom door. An hour later she still hadn't emerged. He called out her name. No response. So he got dressed and left. He didn't expect she'd want to see him again.

But a fortnight later, he'd received a letter from her. It didn't mention his desertion at all. In fact she expressed, in her impeccable handwriting, her love for him. They were married six months later.

The second time they had sex was the day after their wedding. They honeymooned in a little seaside village in Suffolk. On the shingle beach, Hyacinth had stood transfixed by a wrecked old fishing boat on the shore. She turned to Richard and said:

It's nice to be moored.

Richard held his hand out, and she gripped it tight. They went back to their bed and breakfast as the sky turned grey behind them, and they drew the curtains and quietly made love in the dark. Hyacinth lay tight against Richard's side, a warm glow on her face.

Daisy's Toyboy

Daisy drinks alone in a pub. She is watching a young man three tables across: handsome, jutting jaw, Brylcreemed hair, white t-shirt. He couldn't be older than twenty-five. She dreams of their life together.

They would drink several gin and tonics, then go up to one of the small rooms upstairs and make love. After, running her finger through the grooves between his ribs, Daisy would confide in him. Onslow has long since lost interest in her, she would explain, and after these stolen afternoons with him, the stranger, in this dirty bed upstairs at the pub, she feels like a human being again. Daisy would hand him the envelope of cash—the payment to take away Mr White, Rose's lover. He would count it. Daisy would toy with offering the stranger a significant amount of money to be her full-time lover. She would dream of taking out a loan and renting him an apartment. She'd get a job to pay for it.

At closing time, Daisy follows him. The stranger paces in front of the door by the tea shop, the one which leads to Mr White's apartment. Daisy, waiting a safe distance away by the charity shop across the street, hears the door click open and sees a silhouette appear. The two have a conversation, but she can't hear it. Then, the stranger headbutts Mr White, who falls to the ground.

Daisy runs over just as Rose appears in the doorway, dazed, in her dressing gown. Daisy pulls Rose away from the clutches of Mr White and towards her car.

Leaning down over Mr White's hunched body, the stranger gazes up at Daisy across the street, his work done. Daisy starts the car, and the engine backfires, billowing smoke across the street. When the smoke clears, neither the stranger, the unconscious Mr White, nor the car is anywhere to be seen.

The Hostess

Hyacinth hosts Rose and Daisy for afternoon tea, discreetly, in the kitchen, with the ordinary crockery. Rose is distraught. Mr White has left town, without leaving so much as a phone number. She sobs and tells her sisters that Mr White was an angel sent to watch over her.

He was a businessman from Croydon and he's probably gone back to his wife, says Daisy.

No, she tells them, he was literally an angel.

He had a voice perfect like gold, she says, and his tongue tasted of electricity. He sang like a chorus of birds. He came from elsewhere, from the Garden of Eden. He's held unmilled souls in his hands. He told me so, and I've no reason not to believe him.

Hyacinth picks up Rose's teacup and places a coaster underneath it.

Do you know what it is to make love to an angel? says Rose. Do you know how it feels to have those hands on you?

Rose, snaps Hyacinth. I hardly think that's appropriate. Not on my new glazed marble worktop.

Then: a loud bang, as a bird nosedives the window, sliding down the glass to its death.

Country Estate Sale

Hyacinth and Richard attend a Peer's country estate sale. Richard tries to rein in Hyacinth's spending impulses.

Richard picks up a battered silver frame containing a portrait of a gaunt old man.

You think that just because things have belonged to the aristocracy they have some hidden value, says Richard.

Hyacinth isn't listening. She's become fixated on a painting of a boy wearing a suit of green velvet, with a long cape. He stands defiantly against a stormy horizon, one hand on his hip, the other gripping a green bottle by the neck.

A little like Gainsborough's *Blue Boy*, she thinks, a painting she remembers from her art classes at the church hall. She remembers it being described as 'splendid and harmonious'. She says the words aloud, under her breath, like an incantation. *Splendid and harmonious.*

Hyacinth gazes into the boy's eyes, yearning, simple. He reminds her of Sheridan at that age. On his bottom lip, a hint of red. Blood? Or is it something from that green bottle? She has a sudden desire to pull the bottle from his hand and put it to her lips.

When the auction begins, the painting is the first item. Richard forbids her to raise her hand. They can't afford it. The auction continues, but Hyacinth, upset at losing the Boy, has lost her appetite for bidding.

The final item is a lot of six bottles of homemade wine, brewed by generations of Ladies of the House. The auctioneer scoffs at it, joking about its high alcohol content and possible use as a paint remover.

Hyacinth immediately recognises the bottles as the kind the Green Boy was holding. She bids £10 and wins.

She can almost taste it.

Stately Home

ANOTHER MORNING TEA, ANOTHER TRIP TO THE BATHROOM to clean spilt tea from her blouse. Elizabeth is startled to find that the new door next to the bathroom, the one she passed through a few weeks earlier, has suddenly reappeared.

She enters. It's still a hallway, but it's different this time. There are more hallways branching off at intervals down the way. There's a distant hiss somewhere—the sound of wind. She follows it down one of the new hallways, and takes a wrong turn, and before long she has lost herself in labyrinthine corridors. She takes a left, another left, a third left. The halls get narrower, the ceiling lower. Somewhere behind her, she hears Hyacinth's voice, on the phone, talking to Sheridan, slowly dimming to nothing. Elizabeth walks straight for half a mile, stooping under the low ceiling. The corridor narrows, curves, then widens again. The ground beneath her feet seems level, but Elizabeth gets the feeling of depth, of going down.

Finally, she comes to a door. Behind it is a narrow room filled with plants. Elizabeth walks between the branches, into a thicket. The carpet beneath her feet becomes thick with dirt and weeds, and the foliage grows dense. A breeze rustles the leaves. She hears birdsong.

Elizabeth comes out into a forest, the sky the tint of late afternoon. Springtime. Following a trail to the peak of a hill,

Elizabeth looks out over miles of woods. There's a noise to her right. She's not alone.

There's a little boy there, with a bowl cut and a dirty grey shirt. He looks at her, and hands her a firm hard-boiled egg.

Daddy's Accident

WHEN DADDY HEARS THE VOICE, HE THINKS IT MIGHT BE MORNING. The voice calls his name. *Daddy*. The girls must be up and about already, he thinks. He waits for their footsteps, and for the creak of the hull of the houseboat, the throb of his hangover, but none come. *Daddy*. He opens his eyes to the streetlight shining through the grubby window. Dark out still. Not day. He tries to move and remembers his body is frail now, his bones chalky and creaky, and his girls are old ladies themselves.

Daddy!

The voice isn't coming from the door, it's coming from the window. Daddy pulls himself out of bed. Pulling the window open, he leans out and listens for the sound. The voice, *Daddy, Daddy, I need help*, is coming from above him. A girl's voice, from the roof. Hyacinth? It's a warm spring night. Daddy gets out onto the window ledge and eases his way over to the drainage pipe. He grips it with both hands and pulls himself up.

Daddy, come quickly, the voice says, and Daddy groans as he eases his body weight up. Stronger than his girls would have him believe, more spry than the doctors would admit. Mighty enough to shimmy up this skinny birch. Solid enough that his weight is more than the pipe can bear.

*   *   *   *

Daisy wakes first, and knows instinctively. It's Daddy. The roof again. She runs out front in her nightie and slippers and cries out at the prone form on the step.

As the ambulance drives away, Daisy and Rose argue about who has to tell Hyacinth.

Daddy Dreams of Forest

In the ambulance, Daddy dreams of a forest. The sun shines between the beech branches as he approaches the summit. He's limping. Daddy looks down at his best short pants. They're covered in mud, the same mud that broke his fall when he fell from the oak tree. He knows he's going to get a thrashing when he gets home. So he doesn't go home.

The afternoon light is golden when he gets to the peak of the hill. Daddy sits and stares out over the treetops—the ash, birch and holly trees—and listens for the voice. He hears only birdsong. He wishes he had something to eat, then remembers that he came prepared. He reaches into his knapsack and pulls out a hard-boiled egg.

Then he sees a lady, an older lady he doesn't recognise. Thin, blonde, with kind eyes, in a floral dress and a pink cardigan. She stares at him, as if she's trying to work out if he's real or not. She looks pale, in shock. He hands her the egg. Maybe it will help.

Thank you, she says, her hands shaking.

Porcelain Horse

When Elizabeth doesn't come home, Emmet calls Hyacinth. She tells him that Elizabeth left hours ago. She must have got lost, Hyacinth suggests, although their houses are mere feet apart.

Emmet sits on the couch as the sun goes down, staring at the light changing on the porcelain horse statue. Then, at the piano, he scrawls notes for a song for his new musical. He moves the porcelain horse to the top of the piano as he plays. It soothes him. The song flows out. His fingers find the chords easily, and the words envelop them. As the song settles into a structure, he realises he may be composing his masterpiece. He records a demo on his tape recorder.

Playing it back the following morning, he is disappointed to find that it's a minor key dirge with the rhythm of stampeding horses. *Dad-dy*, it goes. *Dad-dy-on-the-shore.*

Emmet calls the police to report Elizabeth missing.

Shoes

HYACINTH, WHO KNOWS WHAT PEOPLE CALL HER, PLANS ANOTHER one of her semi-legendary candlelight suppers. The invite list includes the Mayor, the Archbishop, and several members of the House of Lords. Richard tries to discourage her from inviting some of the more ambitious names on the guest list, but Hyacinth won't be swayed. She sits at her kitchen table addressing envelopes in calligraphic hand, and then, looking into her reflection in the hallway mirror, she recites her everyday mantra: *Today could be the day I'm mistaken for someone important.*

There's a knock at the door. It's a policeman. He asks about Elizabeth, who has gone missing. Hyacinth pulls him indoors before the neighbours see, but asks him to take off his shoes before she lets him past the vestibule.

The last time anyone saw Mrs Warden, says the detective, she was climbing over the fence to come here. You couldn't shed any light on the situation, could you, Mrs—

Bouquet, says Hyacinth. The detective, confused, checks his notes. She's not here, as you can see, says Hyacinth. She's probably just got lost, the poor dear. She's ever so clumsy sometimes. Her nerves go to pieces over the smallest thing.

While he finishes his tea and jots in his notebook, Hyacinth moves his shoes from the vestibule to the outside doormat.

* * * *

Elizabeth follows the boy as he uses a stick to beat them a path through the thicket. The light is almost gone. About an hour ago she took her shoes off, the little black ballerina flats, and threw them in a bush. She's regretting it now. The twigs have torn holes in her stockings, and she feels blood on the soles of her feet.

What's your name? she asks the boy.

Daddy, the boy replies.

Water Hyacinth

Hyacinth steers a little white skiff through a choppy blue-black sea, the clouds hanging deep grey overhead.

Coming towards her, on the horizon: a raft. As it gets closer, she sees that it's Sheridan's bed. Sheridan will be frightened. He won't jump into the water for fear of water snakes. Hyacinth imagines how the poison would course through his blood, turning it to snake jelly. She steers over towards him.

When she reaches him, he is sitting up in bed wearing his blue periwinkle pyjamas and facing the horizon. He doesn't notice her.

Look at Mummy, she says. Now Sheridan, look at Mummy. There are no snakes.

Hyacinth brings her skiff up alongside the mattress and leans across. She grabs his shoulder. He turns and looks at her, blankly. Then he slides out from beneath the sheets and drops into the water. Hyacinth looks around for him, panicked. But he resurfaces, and dives under again in a perfect arc. His body is half Sheridan, half fish. A green connective tissue at his waist joins the two halves. Algae?

The phone rings, waking Richard with a start. Hyacinth stirs back into consciousness.

If it's Sheridan, tell him to wait, she mumbles. Mummy's coming.

Seashell Elizabeth

AT THE EDGE OF THE FOREST, ELIZABETH AND THE BOY REACH A rocky beach. It never gets dark here; it's a perpetual low dusk. Elizabeth looks out over the horizon. The stones chill her feet. She feels something like peace, with the boy, and the ocean.

It's not that I don't like Hyacinth, says Elizabeth. It's just that when I'm in her house I forget where I am. The world seems so far away. I can't orientate myself. And I worry, where is this place? Am I still me? I can't breathe until I'm out the door again.

The boy turns and places his hand on hers, and nods. She feels that he understands. He points. At the end of the beach there's a wrecked ship. They set out towards it, seashells crunching underfoot, his hand in hers. From somewhere, she hears laughter.

The Candlelight Supper

There is no Mayor, no Archbishop, but it's a good turnout at Hyacinth's soirée, especially considering she is under suspicion regarding the disappearance of her neighbour. Mrs Councillor Nugent is there, as are the ancient twins—the two Mrs Pillsworths. Violet and Bruce send their apologies, and a surrogate—a thin man in a grey suit who stands in the corner eating the canapés. The vicar comes, though it's not the vicar Hyacinth invited. This man is much older, redder, balding, with pendulous jowls. She has never seen him before. The room is filled out by a forest of indoor plants, snaking vines, lilies six feet high.

Hyacinth, in a black fascinator, presents to her guests the six bottles of wine she bought at the estate sale. She serves it in glinting crystal glasses. The wine is green—the same green as the boy's velvet coat in the painting—and thick, like syrup. After a supper of roast duck and boiled quail eggs, Hyacinth puts on her Mantovani's Greatest Hits record. The dancing starts. The evening gets blurry. Hyacinth, drunk, gets talking to the Other Vicar. He asks her how long she has lived in this house, and how many rooms it has. In the moment, Hyacinth can't remember.

The record ends. The two Mrs Pillsworths click their fingers in applause, their eyes glazed over with green wine. Then the door bursts open and Elizabeth emerges shoeless and filthy, and promptly faints, dragging a tablecloth and an array of crystalware to the floor with her. From the long, dark hallway, Hyacinth hears the sound of footsteps. She walks towards the door and looks into the blackness. The Other Vicar steps forward and slams the door shut.

You mustn't, he says, his voice sharp with urgency.

The Court of Horses

Richard and Hyacinth are out driving when they see Daddy running naked across the freeway. After sending Richard out into traffic to catch him, Hyacinth directs him to drive to Rose and Daisy's place to return him, but everyone's out. So Hyacinth decides to leave her father with her sister Violet. Again, no one is home. Determined not to have to take Daddy home herself, Hyacinth looks for a way into the house. While she's doing this, Daddy, naked but for Richard's trench coat, escapes over a hedge. Hyacinth follows him through the garden and finds a ladder leaning on a tree. She begins to climb. The audience laughs uproariously, causing the microphones to distort.

The tree seems much larger when she's among its branches. Hyacinth pushes through dense foliage until she comes to a large clear area beneath a thick canopy. It's dark, almost too dark to see, but there are flickering lights all around her. Her eyes adjust. The lights are candles being held by figures, all perched on branches, wearing animal masks and dark feathered cloaks. There's a bird, a cat, three breeds of dog, a frog, a fox. At the summit, on the highest branch, sits a tall figure wearing a horse skull. It stares down at her.

Hyacinthus

THE OTHER VICAR POPS BY UNEXPECTEDLY. HYACINTH SERVES TEA
and the good cream biscuits in the formal sitting room. This Vicar,
unlike the regular one, speaks quickly, and fills any gaps that
Hyacinth might leave. He has come here to speak of Elizabeth, who
was lost in the labyrinthine rooms of Hyacinth's house for some weeks.

Of course, says the Other Vicar, it's not unusual for a house to
have more rooms than you initially thought. The Bible shows us this.
As do many books.

Hyacinth tries to steer the conversation towards more genteel
matters, but the Other Vicar is unshakable.

It works with any book, he explains. Then he walks over to
Hyacinth and Richard's bookshelf. He picks out a hardcover copy of
the Reader's Digest's *A Garden for All Seasons*, lays it flat on the
coffee table, and opens it somewhere in the middle. He puts his
finger on a line without looking, and then reads it aloud:

> *You will know that you have this bee in your garden by*
> *nests in existing hollows, though*

He stops mid-sentence, and turns the pages, rapidly. Another
fragment:

it will circle around to the beginning. Time is

He pauses and flicks the pages, licking his fingertip to get purchase on the paper.

a weed that grows between the stones.

With that he closes the book and smiles. Well, he says, it doesn't work in every book.

After the Other Vicar leaves, Hyacinth gets the book back off the shelf and turns to the glossary of flowers:

> *In Roman Catholic tradition, the hyacinth represents*
> *prudence, constancy, desire of heaven and peace of mind. It*
> *is derived from the story of Hyacinthus, upon whose death*
> *the flower sprang forth.*

Underneath the entry there's a painting of a man cradling a beautiful, dying boy.

Temple of Wood

EACH YEAR HYACINTH MARKS THE ANNIVERSARY OF SHERIDAN'S
death by remembering all the things she never cared for when he
was here. Here he is pulling threads loose from his new pants. Here,
splitting a fat worm on a hook. Here, filling his pockets with damp
soil. Here, burying himself in the garden. Putting roots down, like a
tree, he said. Here, he disappears for two days. Here, he is found in
the thicket at the edge of the golf course, sleeping in a bed of leaves.
Here, his mother cruelly drags him from the earth, scours him clean,
and places him back in his starched white sheets.

Hyacinth builds as clear a picture as she can manage, until it is as
if he could come home any moment now, dragging a heavy spade,
his hands oily from handling something living. Sheridan worshipped
at the forest. He disappeared into the forest any day he could, among
the spires of the trees. Who knows what he got up to? Not
Hyacinth.

It's now, in the spring twilight, that she thinks of him most.

It's dusk and he will come, as long as she keeps an eye on the
clock, as long as she listens for every sound that might be him over
the back fence, as long as she lays a place for him at the table, as long
as she stands by the door and breathes the darkening air, thick with
birdsong. Birds Sheridan might have been able to name. Hyacinth
had made a show of demanding he clean himself up before tea. Why

had she done that? She hadn't minded his grime, his being filthy with life.

Hyacinth realises she is being watched, and sees Elizabeth's face peering blankly out of her front window. She can hear Emmet's deranged piano from behind the glass. Then Elizabeth closes the curtain and disappears.

Rain hits the roof. Slow, fat drops. Hyacinth leaves the door ajar and goes to bed.

Mind Your Manors, Onslow

ONSLOW RECEIVES A LETTER INFORMING HIM OF THE DEATH OF A distant aunt he never knew he had. He has inherited a large manor house, and he, Daisy, Rose, and Daddy move into it.

Onslow's life becomes a nightmare of administration and paperwork. Half his days are taken up just getting around the house. Each room can take minutes to cross, his footsteps echoing across the marble floors. Daisy is pursued around the house by insistent service staff obsessed with spoon-feeding her caviar. Daddy becomes fully mentally cognisant and takes over a wing of the house, working the garden staff like a prison governor. A legal dispute emerges with the deceased aunt's estranged lover, who wants the land, and whom Rose immediately starts lusting after. Onslow begins to suspect the footsteps he hears echoing behind him are not his own.

This episode was never aired.

Hyacinth Richard

THERE ARE THREE HYACINTHS AND THREE RICHARDS IN THE house. Each is an echo of the last, with a delay of between one and five seconds. Hyacinth gets out of bed and turns to see she's still in bed, gets out of bed and turns to see she's still in bed, gets out of bed.

It's like when you call a radio station and don't turn your own radio down, says Richard. He sets up cameras all over the house, hoping to film all six members of the household, but all the video tapes capture is a distorted visual howl.

Eventually the delay extends to an entire day. The couple have to live around echoes of what they were doing yesterday, and the day before. They are disappointed to realise it's almost exactly what they are doing today.

Golfing with the Major

RICHARD IS OUT OF TOWN. ALL HYACINTH WILL TELL ANYONE IS that he's 'golfing with the Major'.

Richard has actually been invited to join a fraternal organisation/cult called the Merchant Clerks. They operate out of a private club in the City, called the Horse-at-Sea. The inside of the building resembles below deck of an old ship, full of narrow wooden halls and low ceilings. In a narrow waiting room, Richard hangs up his coat and waits. A number of young women pass through, all carrying folders of papers, and enter a small side door. None of them have mouths.

A thin, bald man wearing a tie decorated with a pattern of silver keys guides Richard to a boardroom where he is to be interviewed by a panel. The interview may take some days, they explain. He is given the opportunity to call Hyacinth. He explains to her that he is golfing with the Major and he may be some days. Hyacinth is thrilled to hear Richard is golfing with a person of high social standing, and asks him to invite the Major for tea.

When Richard is pushed into a side room while the panel deliberates, he leans over a desk and flicks through some of the piles of paper. They are all covered in thick lines of black ink, horizontal across the page: every single word redacted.

Copper Beech Fever

With Richard still away, Hyacinth dusts every corner of every room. When she is finished, she pours herself a nightcap of the Dowager Lady Ursula's green wine. It's thick and viscous in the glass, shimmering emerald as it catches the light. Hyacinth speaks to camera about the first time she drank alcohol. She stole a bottle of her father's scrumpy and drank it from a sherry glass halfway up a copper beech tree. When Daisy and Violet came looking for her, she fell from her branch, momentarily knocking herself unconscious. She heard then, as she has heard all her life, the bevy of laughing voices baying for her misfortune. She stood up, dusted herself down, and stumbled home, only discovering a few days later that she had given herself a minor concussion.

Hyacinth drifts off to sleep in her bed and awakes somewhere else. The walls creak, the floor shifts. She's aboard the houseboat. Daddy and the others aren't there. Hyacinth looks in the mirror. She's shed forty years. She runs a finger over her clear, soft cheek and smiles. She'll be late for work.

It's a bright, warm day, and the roads are deserted. On the back path by the canal, Hyacinth finds Daddy passed out in the dirt. She can't seem to wake him. In town it's the same. Everyone is asleep, on benches, in cars, on the ground, as if a wave of poison gas had hit the town. In the tea rooms she finds Richard as he was then, young, gormless, and sleeping like a baby. Only Hyacinth is unaffected.

Hyacinth rides her bike to the edge of town, to the copper beech she fell from. There's a body there, exactly where hers landed. But when she gets close enough, she realises it's not her. It's Sheridan, his face swollen with bee stings, his breathing shallow. She picks up his limp body and shakes it, slaps his cheek lightly.

Then she wakes, back in her bed. There's a wine glass on her dresser, with dregs of sickly green liquid. Hyacinth vows to dispose of the rest of the wine once and for all.

Richard at Sea

Richard stares out the port bow window of the Horse-At-Sea. He has been below deck for three days filing paperwork while the man with the key-pattern tie steers the ship through endless choppy seas. One of the mouthless women brings him a cup of tea, and he accepts it wearily. But then, on the horizon, he sees land.

A few hours later he's on a dinghy headed towards a golden beach, fringed by forest. As the sound of crashing waves grows closer, Richard sees that the shoreline is littered with seashells. And the sound isn't just waves—it's the sound of a hundred people laughing.

The sound is coming from inside the seashells.

Var Carridor

AMONG THE BOXES OF SHERIDAN'S THINGS SHE KEEPS UNDER HIS old bed—schoolbooks, toys, drawings—Hyacinth finds a stack of magazines. They are editions of something called *Blue Boy* from the seventies and eighties. Pages and pages of artfully nude men with doe eyes and soft flesh. They must have been for his art classes.

One falls open to a full-page photo of a beautiful boy, chest bare, arms behind his head, his bushy eyebrows arched and his curly hair adorned with devil horns. The photo is sepia-tinted, and looks like it's from the turn of the century. The page is bookmarked with a seed packet. Sweet peas.

Then, she finds Sheridan's secret diary, stuffed behind the dresser. In it, he wrote of a secret world he had created, populated by burly men who have sex with giant flowers. The stories, told across dozens of pages of tiny, cursive script, are colourfully illustrated with the Derwent watercolour pencils Hyacinth had bought him for his tenth birthday. Sheridan's notes go into great detail about copulation, with drawings of penises entwined by plant stamen, and cherub-like newborns wrapped in petal blankets. He named this world Var Carridor.

She is interrupted by the sound of the front door. Richard has been away golfing for several days. Hyacinth is excited to see him. Except it's not Richard. The man hanging his coat in the hallway is dressed like Richard, and has a similar face and the same fine red-grey hair, but he is a stranger. He is taller, his gait is more confident, and his eyes are slightly crossed. Yet the strange man insists that he is Richard. He smiles at her and asks how her day was.

The Garden

Hyacinth finds that as her world becomes smaller, her memories of Sheridan grow more distant. She becomes worried that she can't remember his face. So she tries to draw it. Sitting at the kitchen table with Sheridan's secret diary, she draws face after face, all of them wrong.

The man who isn't Richard has made himself at home. From a distance, Hyacinth thinks, he could be her husband. He is almost Richard. She squints at him, looks at him from the corner of her eye, through parted fingers, and imagines the man she married. But then he moves oddly, loudly clears his throat, or smiles at her in a way Richard never would. He smells strange, like old clay, and he spends most of his days sitting in Richard's armchair watching motor racing on television.

To escape the house, Hyacinth goes for a walk in the nearby nature reserve. She hears a groaning sound in the thicket, and wanders from the path to investigate. Stumbling through the marsh, Hyacinth pulls back the branches and sees a man with his trousers around his ankles, thrusting into a tree. He turns and looks at her, and his face freezes with consternation. Then, as if she isn't there, he turns away and continues thrusting.

Hyacinth turns around and heads home. She tries to draw Sheridan's face again, but the only face she can recall is the man's, contorted in beautiful anguish.

Richard's New Hobby

RICHARD HAS RETURNED HOME FROM HIS NEW CLUB WITH A NEW hobby—he is to become a filmmaker. At first, Hyacinth encourages his newfound artistic interest. He walks the streets, hiding in phone booths and bushes, filming people doing mundane things. Then he spends long hours at his desk editing laugh tracks onto the raw footage.

Hyacinth watches through a crack in the door as he works. He has created an elaborate machine programmed with dozens of different laughs. When played properly, it produces a symphony of reactions from chuckles to raucous howls. A look of intense concentration on his face, Richard sits in the dark, synthesising ecstatic roars of laughter over a video of a woman eating a sandwich in the park.

Richard watches his tapes repeatedly. The footage is funny in its mundanity, and then, upon repetition, not funny. Eventually, he finds, it becomes funny again.

A Picnic For Daddy

Hyacinth and her sisters hold a birthday picnic for Daddy's eighty-fifth birthday. Richard brings his camera. Much to Hyacinth's embarrassment, he films everything for his art project.

When the camera falls on Daddy, he just stares blankly down the lens. Daddy remembers being filmed when he was young. It was the day the men came back from France. There was a man in town from the War Office, lugging a huge black camera on stilts. The ghostly soldiers walked ashen-faced up the streets, and their wives and families waved their handkerchiefs, and the man from the War Office pointed the box at them all. Daddy remembers thinking that the machine was going to remember them like this forever: they were frail, scared, ragged, and thin. Like skeletons.

Afterwards, the man pointed the camera at Daddy and some of the other kids. Daddy had never seen a film, and he didn't understand moving pictures. He walked into frame, stood still, posed, while the camera remembered him. *Capture me*, he thought to it.

I'll be still for you. Catch me.

Copse Memory

Hyacinth is seeing echoes of her younger self around the house again. She is always just around the corner, just out of sight.

One night, Hyacinth hides outside Sheridan's bedroom with her ear against the door, listening to her younger self tell Sheridan a nursery rhyme about a very tall man with legs that are five feet long. She remembers that moment. She remembers that Sheridan cried that night because he couldn't sleep, concerned about how the tall man gets around day-to-day.

The following day she hears the post drop. Young Hyacinth collects it. It's the brochure from the school. Hyacinth remembers this too. She was excited by what a good education could do for her son.

But the *fees*, says Young Richard. Young Hyacinth argues that a boy needs discipline, needs something only an exclusive school can provide. She imagines him becoming something more than her, something real.

Hyacinth remembers she was secretly terrified of letting Sheridan go. Young Hyacinth dreams of shrinking him down and putting him in a pouch of her flesh, a warm, mucousy fold in her belly. She never told Richard about that dream.

The phone rings, but Hyacinth misses it, thinking it's just another echo.

The Black Milk

HYACINTH DREAMS THAT SHE AND RICHARD MYSTERIOUSLY inherit a mansion in the country. The estate is two hundred acres, with gardens, stables, and a private lake. It will not be simple to maintain, but for Hyacinth, it's the culmination of her destiny. She is ready to throw herself into becoming one of the landed gentry.

Elizabeth visits for afternoon tea. They welcome Elizabeth graciously, and show her to the parlour. But Elizabeth sees that Hyacinth is living a lie, that she is seeing it all wrong: the estate is, in fact, an abandoned farmhouse, partially collapsed, thick with damp, dense fog. Elizabeth breaks it to Hyacinth gently—it's an illusion. Hyacinth immediately sees as Elizabeth sees. In a filthy mirror, she sees herself and Richard looking deathly ill, but oblivious to their surroundings. They drink brown water from a trough, and sleep in a bed of leaves. The service staff, a trio of spindly men in suits made of straw, are serving an afternoon tea of mouldy bread stuffed with pungent weeds and mugs of foul black liquid.

Hyacinth throws her cup of black milk to the floor, and the three of them escape back to town.

When Hyacinth wakes from her dream, she resents Elizabeth's interference. Her new life was a lie, but she was happy.

Trees, Babies, Oceans

Feeling sorry for Richard being stuck at home with Hyacinth all day, Emmet takes him out to the pub. Over warm pints of bitter, Emmet realises that it's he who needs to unwind. He's been unable to compose for almost a year. The songs he does manage to write are unlistenable, experimental pieces about trees, babies, oceans. Completely unsuitable for his musical, which is a comedy about a butler who inherits a mansion.

Richard tells Emmet that he needs to allow the project to be what it wants to be. He tells him about his experimental film, about the way the laughter washes over the trivialities and sorrows of his subjects, rendering each problem the same, wearing them down to nothing.

Maybe babies and trees and oceans is the story you need to tell, says Richard. Stories often aren't just our own.

Young Elizabeth

New to the area, Elizabeth goes next door to introduce herself to her neighbour. The woman answers the door in distress. She has received a phone call that her son Sheridan has been in an accident at school. It's eighty miles away, and she can't drive, and Richard isn't answering the phone at work, and she doesn't know what to do. Elizabeth offers to drive her where she needs to go. Hyacinth says that it's eighty miles, it's too far, but Elizabeth insists.

They drive in silence, Hyacinth looking at her watch every minute, Elizabeth speeding nervously. When they arrive at the school, a huge Georgian mansion, Elizabeth sits outside the headmaster's office listening

The Whole Boy

Old Hyacinth answers the phone. There's no one there, just the buzz of static. 'Sheridan,' she says, a broad smile crossing her face. For twenty years Hyacinth has carried on a conversation with her son in this way, though he never responds. Hyacinth believes that if she never loses his voice from her memory, she will never lose his face. If she never loses his face, she will never entirely lose him. These two beacons are all she needs to summon the whole boy, to spark his consciousness back to life whenever she needs.

She has aged him in her mind from the last time she saw him, stretched him, deepened his features, thickened his brows, knitted a manly stubble across his face. So close she can touch him, to Hyacinth crying, shouting. A secretary offers Elizabeth a cup of tea. Her hands are shaking too much to hold it without spilling it. After an hour, the secretary assures Elizabeth that Richard is on the way, and she drives home alone, her hands shaking on the steering wheel.

When she arrives home, Elizabeth sees lights on at Hyacinth's. She knocks on the door, but there's no answer. She peers in the window. There's an old woman in there, perhaps Hyacinth's mother—she looks very similar, though decades older. The woman looks back at her, slowly raises her hand, and waves.

feel his warmth, see him just out of the corner of her eye, digging a hole in the garden with his hands. His voice is lower, fuller, as if coming from somewhere deeper in him, and so real she can hear, down the phone, faint but real. She wonders if Richard has an image of their son like this, but she doesn't have the courage to ask.

When it gets dark out, Hyacinth sees a face at the lounge room window. It's Elizabeth, and she looks exactly as she did that day, and she's crying still too. She stands frozen at the window for a moment, her tears still as glue.

Daisy Wheel

WHEN ROSE WAKES, SHE IMMEDIATELY REMEMBERS HER DREAM: she was deep in a green sea, swimming away from a spinning wheel of burning human heads, each bearing the face of her sister Daisy. She was reaching for the phosphorescent surface, the flames licking at her feet.

She sits up in bed and reaches for her diary, writes down *Daisy wheel*, and tears out the page. Rose has taken to writing down things that frighten her and keeping them close. The closer she keeps it, the quicker the thing loses its power. She scrunches the torn page into a ball and tucks this one into her nightie, by her heart.

Daisy wakes before dawn and shuffles to the bathroom. There, at the other end of the hall: it's Rose. She's on the landing by her door in one of her extravagant nighties, smoking a cigarette and staring out the window at the moon. What's she doing up at this time? When Rose sees Daisy, she quickly stubs out her cigarette on the window sill and retreats to her room. There's a rustling sound as she walks, as if her clothes are made of paper.

The Toy Shop

Young Hyacinth takes difficult child Sheridan to a toy shop. She is hoping to find him a hobby, anything to keep him inside and in her sight. While Hyacinth explains to the cashier that her son is passionate about nature and precociously intelligent, Sheridan inspects an elaborate model train set, watching it course though a tabletop landscape of farmland, trees, roads. Sheridan gets up on a stool to get a view from above. The forest is a maze of twigs. Farms are neat patchwork rugs. Towns are little monopoly houses scattered on the uneven ground in winding rows. Sheridan is a giant. He reaches out and touches the river. It's frozen. As the train starts to pass, he reaches out and holds it in place, its wheels whirring, the engine vibrating pleasantly through his hand, up his arm. There's a boy in the forest. In among the trees, a little figurine of a boy. Sheridan clambers onto the table to get a closer look. The world gives way beneath him.

Young Hyacinth pulls Sheridan from the wreckage unscathed and leaves the shop with a bill for several hundred pounds.

Twenty years later, Old Hyacinth passes by the shop and hears the crash of the train, the level crossing signal ding-ding-dinging in her ears, the passengers crying out for their loved ones, and feels the ground shaking beneath her feet.

New Daddy

Reviewing the footage he recorded at Daddy's birthday picnic, Richard notices something odd. The normally absent Daddy seems stronger, sharper. He observes quietly, carefully as people look straight past him. Even when he speaks, people ignore him.

Richard rewinds over a moment when Daddy looks fondly on as Hyacinth fusses over a spilt salad. He rewinds again, and then again. The fourth time he watches it, Daddy turns and looks right at him.

Angel Angel Angel

At night Rose slips out to the garden shed, where she keeps the baby.

Among the cobwebs, disused plant pots and old Christmas decorations is a basket containing a grey blanket. Rose pulls the blanket back, and the baby blinks warmly at her. A twisted mass of flesh, pulsing, breathing, eyes, limbs and fur protruding from every conceivable angle. The camera never settles on it for long. It looks different in every shot, grotesque and beautiful at the same time, and its skin has a radiant glow.

The baby tells her, leaves impressions on her mind, that it must remain a secret, at least for now.

Angel angel angel, Rose whisper-sings to it, stroking its fur and flesh as she feeds it its bottle. *Baby baby baby*. The baby is soothed, and so is Rose.

Rose sits on the little stool by the shed and rocks the baby gently. She doesn't really remember the pregnancy. It was like a dream. Perhaps it was a dream. When she tries, she can't even remember how long she's been tending the child. A week, perhaps a year. New mothers experience this slip of memory, she tells herself—when the child arrives it's as if it's always been there. She doesn't ever remember wanting children, but now that it's here, and it's hers, she is in love.

Copse Memory Two

Richard and Hyacinth's house is fast filling up with mysterious foliage. First, a houseplant doubles in size overnight. By the next day, the garden is an unruly wilderness. Then, entire rooms are consumed by vines growing from the wainscoting, from the power points, from the light fittings. Richard takes to it all with industrial-strength weed killer, but it always returns the next day. Hyacinth's wallpaper is completely ruined.

Hyacinth begins to notice that flowers are growing behind her wherever she walks. Little patches of garden in the exact shape of her footsteps.

The Mayor's Fancy Dress Ball

Hyacinth and Richard aren't invited to the Mayor's masquerade ball, but Hyacinth insists they go anyway. They'll sneak in. No one will know who they are underneath their masks, she reasons.

Hyacinth dresses as a sparrow. Richard is a wolf.

The ball is held in a huge banquet hall attached to the local church. Hyacinth quickly loses Richard in the sea of animal silhouettes. A fish offers her a glass of green wine. It's hard to make people out by candlelight. The one person she recognises is the Other Vicar, still wearing his collar. He has come as a Cro-Magnon man. Hyacinth admires his mask: the strong, brooding paleolithic jawline.

The table is overfull with greenery. When Hyacinth gets closer, she sees that it's not flowers, but arrangements of weeds and shrubs, pulled straight from the ground, complete with great clumps of dirt on the white linen tablecloth.

While she is sneaking a canapé under her mask, a man dressed as an ibis strikes up a conversation. Have you seen the child? he asks, his long beak spiking her shoulder. Will the child be here tonight? Hyacinth doesn't know what to say. Her canapé tastes of dirt.

A hush falls across the room. At the head of the banquet table, a man in a horse skull directs people to take their seats. There's a flurry of movement as the crowd quickly find their places and sit, leaving just the sparrow and the wolf standing alone. The other animals turn and stare.

Green Narthex

Hyacinth suspects that the plants that have been growing freely inside her house are trying to communicate with her. While Richard potters in the garden, she pulls some weeds from under the skirting board and lays them out on the kitchen table. She whispers:

Sheridan … Sheridan can you hear me?

She lays her ear to the table and listens patiently. But she hears nothing but the dull yawn of the varnished wood.

When Richard comes in from the garden, he doesn't say anything about the table covered in weeds and earth, or ask why Hyacinth's head is buried amongst it. He simply asks her: Why does the same hearse keep going round and round?

Hyacinth follows him to the front garden. She knows the hearse. She expects it. But as it comes around yet again, Richard points. A sleek black glacier of a vehicle approaches, driverless, silent.

Rose dreams that Hyacinth is trying to kill her and take away her secret baby. In her dream, a car speeds towards her. The last thing she sees is Hyacinth in the passenger seat, her hand over Richard's eyes as the car mounts the pavement.

Guf

Elizabeth and Emmet attend a committee meeting for the upcoming Pageant. They go to great lengths to exclude Hyacinth from the arrangements, leaving the house under cover of darkness, long after the last lights have gone out at the Bucket household.

The church hall is a hive of activity. Emmet sits at the piano in the corner and practices the piece he's written especially for the occasion. It's a low, atonal rumble, over which he shrieks and cries like a baby.

Elizabeth, in charge of the wreath, is assigned a helper—a tall, pale man in a grey suit. He smiles through yellow teeth and introduces himself as Mr White. They chat as they weave daisies into the wreath. He has the softest voice Elizabeth has ever heard, and an unplaceable accent. She asks where he is from.

He explains that he is from the Garden, where he watched over the Guf, the Treasury of Souls. His job used to be to select the souls to be born, before passing them to Lailah, the Angel of Conception, who cared for the embryos until they were born into the world.

That sounds like a lot of responsibility, says Elizabeth.

It was! says Mr White, with an exaggerated sigh and a laugh. But, he shrugs, now I am here.

On his tea break, Mr White peers through the blinds into the car park. She's still there. Rose, beneath the glow of a street-light, wearing a frilly pink dress with puffy sleeves, idly rocking a pram. A cigarette hangs from the side of her mouth, blowing blue smoke into the yellow light. The figure in the pram has outgrown it. Over the sides hang the bare legs and feet of an adolescent.

The Pageant

WHEN HYACINTH WAKES, RICHARD ISN'T THERE. SHE'S SURPRISED to find that she's slept in. Now that the hedge by the window has completely consumed the front of the house, no light comes through the curtains.

The air throughout the house is still. After getting dressed and making breakfast, Hyacinth stands on the front doorstep in her nightgown, waiting for some sign of life, but there's nothing. She steps over the low brick fence and knocks on Elizabeth and Emmet's door. She calls Elizabeth's name.

Coffee at eleven, Elizabeth? she calls out, but there's no answer.

Hyacinth hears in the distance the sound of a crowd—a festival, or a carnival. The sound gradually swells, until it's a street away. It's a horrible din, an atonal clamouring of piano and voice, adorned with rhythmic shrieking. Around the corner comes a black hearse, followed by dozens of chanting revellers, some with tambourines, some with brass instruments. She recognises each of them. There's Bruce, in his horse costume. And Richard, dressed as a wolf. The Other Vicar, in his caveman get-up, greets her politely and points to the back of the hearse. The rear door hangs open. From somewhere comes the sound of laughter.

Beside her, dressed in a skeleton suit, is Daddy. He looks at her, more present than she's seen him in years. He points beyond. She turns to see Rose, in a black dress and veil, waving. She's with a strange man. She's pushing a pram with an adult man sitting in it. He stands, thin, naked, and walks towards Hyacinth. He's a foot taller than her, young and beautiful and silent. He has a face Hyacinth has never seen before, or hasn't seen in years. She begins to cry, and embraces him. The laughter grows into applause. Richard pulls off his mask, presents her with a bunch of limp flowers, and kisses her warmly on the cheek. With a final goodbye, Hyacinth clambers into the back of the hearse, and takes her place in the waiting coffin. The crowd cheers.

Daddy takes the lead, wandering slowly up the street, breaking out into a little dance as he goes. The hearse follows. As it rolls slowly through the crowd, Hyacinth waves through the window: to the Other Vicar, to Emmet, to Violet, Daisy and Onslow, to Bruce-As-Horse, to Rose, to Skeleton Daddy, to Elizabeth, and to Sheridan.

The credits roll.

The Wild Hive

Twilight, a forest. Something twitches among the branches. It's Hyacinth. Her blue floral dress is torn and grubby, but her eyes are bright.

For the first weeks, berries and acorns sustained her. As she grew accustomed to her new surrounds, she summoned more and more strength. Now she sleeps in a bed of dry leaves, and the earth gives her food. She has learned the difference between the good flowers and the bad flowers. The root that will make her strong, and the weed that will make her sick. The forest is peaceful and alive, just as Sheridan knew it was. She should have listened.

There's a sound, but it's not the one she's been listening for. It's a hum all the same, and one that has haunted her. She scales a mossy tree to the source. A hive, a teeming teardrop-shaped growth clinging to the branch. It was bees that took Sheridan away. They marked him as a threat and swarmed him, sucking the breath from his body. A misunderstanding. Now, they crawl up Hyacinth's arm. She isn't frightened. She doesn't want their honey. She pays her tribute and they wish her well on her quest.

Back on the ground, Hyacinth turns, alert. She's heard it, the low rumble in the distance. It's always been there, low enough that she has learned to tune it out, but now it's clear.

She is in tune with the pitch of running water.

Hyacinth walks through the night towards the sound—though she no longer has any sense of time. Time is the weed that grows between the stones. The garden, the whole garden, is what matters. The water is what matters.

She reaches a stream at dawn. Kneeling down, she places her hands in the flow and brings a palmful of water to her mouth. It's cold. Fresh. She feels the flowing stream, and hears its laughter.

Hyacinth follows the stream. Slowly, the flow of water gets thicker. The banks grow wider, further apart. The pace quickens from a gentle pull to a thundering current. By sundown, she can barely make out the other bank at all. There's nothing but the sharp line of horizon, and the rolling ocean of laughter.

She stands ankle-deep first, then deeper, until her legs are numbed by the cold. Until she's sure. Finally, she leaves her clothes on the riverbank and wades in.

She gives herself over to the surge of water, until her head is under, until her feet no longer touch the mossy river floor, until she can no longer see, until the noise subsides, and there's only water.

And bee stings. And candlelight, and Royal Doulton, and Daddy, and Horsehair.

And Sheridan.

And then nothing but cool, deep water.

ACKNOWLEDGEMENTS

Hyacinth originally went out as a weekly email newsletter. So thanks to everyone who subscribed to that, especially the people who responded every week with 'oh!' and 'weird!', and things of that nature.

Thank you to Anna Thwaites for thorough editing and support, Paul Cumming for designing the launch poster, and Fi Wright for her help launching the book.

Thanks and apologies to Roy Clarke, whose BBC sitcom *Keeping Up Appearances* looped endlessly through my childhood. Thanks to Patricia Routledge, Clive Swift, Josephine Tewson and the rest of the cast for providing the voices for this book. Thanks to Mum and Dad for never switching the TV off.

And thanks to Charlotte Ivey, for everything. These pages would be blank without you xxoxx

WILL COX is a lutruwita-born, Naarm-based writer. His short fiction and poetry has appeared in *New Australian Fiction 2022*, *Island*, *Verge*, *Visible Ink*, *Slow Canoe*, and other publications.

will-cox.com